Seven Tales to Redemption 1:

The Green Ladies

by Clark Omo

I. Blood Mixed with Whiskey

Blood mixed with the whiskey well. The floor of the Golden Times Saloon was covered with them both. The killing had been easy; nothing but a bunch of joy juice-hooked yacks who didn't know their guns from their cocks. But catching the damn idiots had been a challenge; they'd gone far and fast, the Gordy Thomas Gang. But here they all lay; bodies chock-full of holes with red leaking out of them like they were beer-barrels. They'd been dead not but a few minutes. Enough time for their killer to light his cigarette, wipe their blood from his face with an already dirty rag, and take a seat across from the reason the men had to die in the first place.

"Jack Dance," said the killer, "been looking a while for you."

Dance smiled, his curling mustache rising with his mouth. In many ways, he was just like all the papers and wanted signs printed him; handsome, roguish, sly, debonair, with that oily smooth and dark-tanned skin, shadow-black hair that, even after all the gory mess was done, stubbornly remained perfect. The creamy brown eyes, known for charming young maids into giving up their baubles, smiled back at the killer with unabashed defiance; he didn't seem consider much that his life was in the balance. The killer saw there a pride: the pride of man who'd set himself on a hilltop of moral superiority. He could see now why the common-folk had crowned him as a hero with such a hard-to-hate face and propensity to rob the rich. As the saying went, one man's outlaw was another man's hero. But all outlaws were the same to the killer, no matter what mask they wore or game they played to get their reputation. The only thing that mattered to the killer when it came to outlaws was the haul they were worth; which was why he'd gone after the Gordy Thomas Gang in the first place; they had Dance.

Dance chuckled. "Well, I wasn't exactly running with the intention of being caught."

The killer put the cigarette in his mouth and let out a few puffs. He said nothing. He just let the flame from the little cigarette light up his shadowed face under his black hat, the embers making the stark white hairs of his beard glow like hot snow. The necklace of sharp, ivory teeth around his neck twinkled, along with the long fang hanging from his ear. The ruby eyes of the black snake heads tattooed on the back of his hands, just barely visible under the edge of his black, rolled-up shirtsleeves, glittered. And the killer's own eyes glared. One green, and the other red.

Dance indicated the carnage. "I suppose this is the part where you clamp my hands and feet and take me to Harristown to collect?"

The killer took the cigarette from his mouth. "Nope."

"Ah. Then Clantonburg?"

"You're getting colder, highwayman," the killer said.

Dance's look of amusement faded away. "Then where?"

The killer said nothing for few moments. Dance boiled. "Where, damn you!?"

The killer made a little chuckle. He leaned closer. "Redemption."

The look on Dance's face told the killer that the thief didn't understand. "Why Redemption?"

"You know why, Dance. You took something that didn't belong to you but did belong to the city of Redemption. And in the ruckus and smoke, you killed six men. You've done a lot of stuff, Dance, thieving and raiding wise. Harassing the Gravesend Trail, robbing the First Chisolm Bank in Capernaum. But now you've

gone and took the cake this time. The good folk of Redemption put a price bigger than Golgotha on your head. *That's* what I plan on collecting."

The killer threw the cigarette to the saloon's floor and stamped it out in a pool of gore.

Dance blinked. "Big as Golgotha, you say? How big is that, exactly?"

"Fifty thousand," the killer said.

"Fifty…" The thief's eyes went wider than the sky. "That much…for what I took? It can't be."

"It is," the killer said.

"But—that means that half the Wilds will be looking for me…" Dance said, suddenly devoid of gusto. His eyes started moving from side to side rapidly. The killer could practically see the synapses lighting up a firework show as Dance tried to figure his way out of this. It made him smile.

"You got it right there, outlaw. Which means that Gordy Thomas over yonder." The killer pointed to a dead man lying on the bar's top with a pair of glass shards sticking from his throat. "Won't be the only yahoo looking to scalp you and take that prize. You are wanted dead or alive, you know."

Dance laughed bitterly. "Let me guess. The reward's bigger if I'm taken alive, is that it?"

The killer lit another cigarette. "Exactly. And you'd better be glad I took the precious time to notice that minute detail."

The killer got up from the table and hauled Dance to his feet. They walked out the door into the sun and dusty street. A crowd had gathered in front of the saloon: men, women and children. Even the town marshal, whose mouth was gaping

like everyone else's.

"Thomas and his gang are dead, Marshal," the killer said.

The marshal, a man whose skin had barely a scar worn into it from the sun, stuttered as he spoke, "M—Mister Hawthorn—"

"No need to thank me. It was a pleasure doing your job for you."

The killer pushed Dance onto a horse, then mounted his own black steed.

And they rode off.

II. Settling Differences

Hawthorn. That was his name. And it was not unknown in the land of dangers and beauties, mysteries and riches, killers and outlaws named The Wilds. He was a bounty hunter, a gun for hire. And he rode across these savage and mystical reaches with not a fear nor worry upon his mind, for his blood ran hot with the sun as did the sands, his eyes gleamed sharp like the hawk's, and his aim sped quick and true as the wind.

The Wilds held many things. Wide plains of dry, yellow grass checkered with sparse dogwood and brush, and scorched, merciless deserts dotted with mesas and plateaus and mountains. It was across the plains that Hawthorn now rode, his black rifle slung over his shoulder and a rope fastened to his wrist by which he hauled Dance along by the saddle of the thief's horse.

"I suppose I should thank you, Mister Hawthorn," Dance said.

"For what?" Hawthorn said.

"For saving me, that is, from those wily degenerates. I'm quite sure if that Thomas animal had had his way, I would be missing my fingers as well as my manhood."

"Well, you're mighty welcome. Now, shut your jab and enjoy the scenery. It's the last sights you'll get of such."

"And what is that supposed to mean?"

Hawthorn looked over the wide plains as the low sun turned the yellow grasses to masses of waving wands of gold. "Think on it," he said.

"They mean to hang me in Redemption?"

"It's what I'd do," Hawthorn said, "especially for what you pulled. Killing

those men in cold blood. You took six men from their families."

Dance couldn't restrain his boiling tones. "Oh, don't go and take the high-ground on me, bounty hunter. Me killing those men, in self-defense I might add, while they were serving an establishment that has for years provided for its own interests rather than those of its workers and their families, is nothing compared to a man who'll hogtie another man and take him to certain death for what amounts to blood-money."

Now Hawthorn laughed. It wasn't a sound that Dance found particularly pleasant.

"You'd better find another way of justifying murder instead of equating it with me."

That got Dance angry. "If what I did was murder, then how is it any different from killing a man just because he has a price put on his head? You've no conscience, Hawthorn, any more than you believe that I lack—"

Hawthorn yanked the horse's rope forward, causing the animal to lurch up to him. And suddenly Dance was looking right into the hunter's mismatched eyes.

"Every man I ever killed was a for a reason. You didn't have to be there, Dance. But you were, and you killed men who didn't have it coming. Now, I'm a lot of things, thief. But you and I ain't nothing alike," he growled. The light from that cigarette looked hellish when coupled with the green eye and red eye.

Dance said nothing else.

III. Sleight of Hand

The path Hawthorn had chosen took them to the banks of a shallow water hole shaded by a pair of big oaks. Hawthorn dismounted and led the horses to the water. He let Dance off his saddle to take a swig from a canteen.

"Thank you," Dance said.

Hawthorn turned away and leaned up against one of the oaks. He had a few swallows himself before slipping his cigarette between his lips. Never once did he take his eyes off the thief.

"Half the bounty requires I return with it is whatever you took," Hawthorn said.

"Of course, it does," Dance said, before taking another swig.

"You're going take me to it," Hawthorn said.

"Undoubtedly," Dance said, then handed the canteen back to Hawthorn. "I need to take a piss."

Hawthorn nodded. Dance got to his feet and went to the neighboring oak. Hawthorn kept his gaze fixed on the man. Dance noticed.

"Oh, so I've lost the right to privacy, is that it?"

Hawthorn's response was a puff of smoke and the edging of his finger closer to the rifle's trigger.

Dance scoffed out a chuckle. "Fine." As his hands went to his zipper, he pulled a sleight of hand with all the finesse of an experienced thief. They went to his trouser pocket and pulled out, if Hawthorn had seen it, a small shred of a pale, bluish-green plant. As he bent down to fish out his organ, he crunched and sprinkled the plant bits into the watering hole.

He bent back up quickly to relieve himself. He finished with a satisfied sigh before making himself decent again.

"Time to ride," Hawthorn said.

They mounted their horses and set off again.

* * *

"What was it you took from Redemption?" Hawthorn said.

The thief shifted in his saddle. At any moment now the locoweed would take effect.

"Don't know."

Hawthorn twisted round. "What?"

"I don't know what it is."

"What do you mean you 'don't know'?"

"That's exactly what I mean. I. Don't. Know."

"You mean to tell me you risked your life and got yourself nabbed by Gordy Thomas all over something that you don't even what in living Hell is?"

"Don't make it sound like I'm an imbecile, Hawthorn. It was under heavy guard where I found it in that Tritonium facility. Things that are under that much security usually possess some kind of exquisite value."

Hawthorn chuckled.

Dance scowled. "I'm getting tired of you laughing at jokes I do not intend."

"You thieves. It's wondrous to me how much of ya'll are the same. Ya'll always jump at what looks like the biggest buck like bitches in heat once it crosses

your snouts, even if you haven't got a clue what it might be."

"Hmm. Much like bounty hunters."

That only made Hawthorn laugh more. "I reckon so!"

At that moment the hunter's horse started bucking. "What in—" he clutched the reins as the horse whined, its big and strong back bolting into the air, legs kicking high. Dust clouds billowed. Hawthorn dug his spurs in the animal's side, yanking the reins.

"Calm down, damn it!" he muttered.

Then Dance's horse started. The thief clutched the horse's mane with his hands and dug his spurs in too, hanging for dear life. The rope with which Hawthorn had guided Dance's horse whipped and jerked, finally yanking the hunter right out of his saddle. Then Dance's horse raced ahead in full gallop, overtaking Hawthorn's horse and dragging the bounty hunter in the dust behind it.

Hawthorn rolled his tongue to the back of his mouth, careful not bite down on it as his body raced over the dusty earth. Sand and rocks grated against his shirt and into his skin. Grass whipped him in the face. He couldn't see. His hat flew off his head, exposing his white mane.

He growled. His leg struck a rock stuck fast in the ground. Pain shot up and down his thigh. He reached for his knife, his big knife, and cut the rope with a single swipe. He rolled over the grass for a few feet, his leg getting more agitated with every impact. Finally, his momentum slowed and he went to a stop. He grunted, gritted his teeth and rolled onto his back.

Dance, meanwhile, had gotten a good distance away. Sure, the horse was racing like the wind and he had little to no control over the crazed thing, but he was still getting away. That's what mattered. The taste of freedom was already budding on his tongue. He laughed so the birds could hear him.

Not if Hawthorn could help it. He got to his knees, painfully, begrudgingly, and unslung the rifle from his back. Growling with a Devil's vengeance, he took aim with the black rifle, drawing a bead on the escaping convict. His prey.

Though the sun glared and his knee hurt, he kept his aim steady. The thief was riding fast, and the horse's furious galloping was kicking dust up in the air as to shroud his shape. But he was riding west, giving Hawthorn a clear angle on his intended target. The bounty hunter lined the tip of the sight up right where he wanted it. He fired.

One moment Dance was laughing with his mouth wide, the next he was choking on blood that wasn't his. Hawthorn's bullet had brained the horse. The blood exploded from the poor creature's head, glistening as it painted the grass and Dance's face. The creature stopped midstride, the momentum of the sudden stop hurtling Dance face-first into the dirt. He managed to choke up some soil before a crushing weight landed on his chest. The horse's corpse pinned him where he lay.

Hawthorn stood and started limping over to the waylaid thief. He found his hat lying in the grass a few feet away. He put it on, then took the time to wrap and light a new cigarette.

Dance coughed and spluttered out bits of dirt and horse flesh. The sun glared down at him, its violent brightness nearly blinding him. He felt all its heat on his face. He wanted to wipe the gore from his mouth, but his hands were pinned under the dead horse as well. He did what he could by spitting into the dirt.

He started to move, wriggling himself out from under the thing. No good.

Then a dark shape blotted out the sun. Hawthorn stood over him like the grim visage of an ominous, damning spirit. His eyes glowed, green and red.

"I got to admit that was slick, Dance."

"I'm so—flattered—by your veneration," Dance said, finding it hard to breathe.

Hawthorn took a long drag, and then sprinkled some of the ash on the horse's corpse. Dance heaved out a gasp.

"Let me spell it straight for you, Dance. Those idiots I killed back there in North Crown, Gordy's Gang, were a bunch of ignorant, self-indulgent louts. They didn't know a good job even if it came up and kicked them between the legs. If I hadn't found you before they got to the next town, you would be a feast for maggots. See, they didn't care about taking you alive, even if you meant more money. Putting up with live prey means trouble, and a lot of other hunters wouldn't put up with it, neither. Me, I like to think of myself as a somewhat tolerant man. I'll get you back to Redemption in one piece. You can bank on that, because I like my money. But if you go and pull another trick like the former, I'll skin you, hang your body over a tree branch like a pair of long-johns and let you drip until you're dry. Savvy?"

The thief nodded, his face going red. "Understood," he wheezed.

"Good. Cause from here on, you're walking," Hawthorn took another drag and turned his back.

"Wait!" Dance called.

Hawthorn stopped.

"Aren't you going to help me out from under here?"

The bounty hunter shrugged. "I figure since you so righteously got yourself under that horse's ass, you can sure find your own way out."

And he walked away to find his black horse.

IV. News in Gideonville

Gideonville wasn't half as grand it wanted to sound. It was a medium sized town, situated in the middle of nowhere like most towns past the Fringe Line were. Small cattle trails crisscrossed its roads, and a ranch or two spotted its borders. But for the most part it was just another town, nothing big and nothing small. But it was here that Hawthorn decided to rest. He parked his steed by the marshal's office, dismounted and hitched his horse.

Dance collapsed to his knees, having been pulled by his hands for the last ten miles. Blood ran down his chafed wrists and sweat oiled his face. Hawthorn dismounted and let him have a draught from the canteen. The thief took the little bottle like it was made of gold. He went to his knees and drank until the canteen was empty.

"Don't go nowhere," Hawthorn said, tossing him another canteen.

The outlaw drank greedily. In the meantime, Hawthorn payed the sheriff a visit.

The sheriff himself wasn't anything like the one back in North Crown. He was aged and weathered; his skin rough like sun-squelched leather. His sharp eyes looked Hawthorn down from top to bottom, sizing the bounty hunter up. He put down the set of papers in his hands and stood.

"Morning."

"Morning," Hawthorn said, lighting a cigarette.

"What can I do you for?" the sheriff said, still looking Hawthorn over.

"I've got a fugitive I need you to corral for me. At least 'til dawn."

"What's his name?" said the sheriff, tightening his belt.

"Jack Dance."

The sheriff looked at him. "Jack Dance? *The* Jack Dance? The Highwayman of the Sycamore Trail?"

"Yeah."

"The one that robbed that Clements train way back when?"

"Bull's eye."

"The one with the fifty-thousand-dollar haul on his head from Redemption?"

"The same."

The sheriff shook his head and holstered his six-shooter. "I—I can do that. And who am I holding him for?"

"Me."

"And your name?"

"Hawthorn."

Again, that made the old sheriff pause. "Let me guess...*The* Hawthorn?"

"The one and only."

"Should've known. Those eyes." Then the sheriff laughed and went back to his chair. "Well, I'll be stuffed like a turkey and call my daddy a greyskin. First the Green Ladies, and now *the* Hawthorn shows up with *the* Jack Dance on my porch step. Those are some hell of some omens."

Now it was Hawthorn's turn to be surprised. "The Green Ladies? Here?"

"As sure as I'm old and my knees ache. You didn't see their floating garden or whatever coming into town?"

"I didn't."

"Well, it's got its blue anchor in the sand on the other end of town. Their Headmistress, Lillian, I think, had to set it there after she got in a spat with the mayor and the colonel in charge of the cavalry brigade here. Said they didn't want no prim and proper harlot house poisoning the good folk of this town or the soldiers. She argued back she was a legitimate business, and all the accusations and such of her girls being harlots was poppycock. So, they made her set up shop on the outskirts." The sheriff paused to scratch his white beard. "Funny. Now that I think about it, I saw the mayor heading in that direction this morning."

"There's a garrison stationed here?"

"Yeah. The ranchers have been getting raided by the Neotok. Damned savages nearly wiped out a whole herd of good steers last month."

"Who's the colonel in command?"

"Name's Gordonson."

Hawthorn knew that name. The sound of it brought a foul taste to the back of his mouth.

"Well, about time I see the criminal." The old sheriff got up, his knees popping as he did so. "By the way, Hawthorn, name's Rodham McGuire," he said, extending his hand.

"Obliged," Hawthorn said, and shook his hand.

The two went outside to find Dance on his knees and his head resting against the horse's rump. His hair and face were drenched, and the two empty canteens lay on the dirt. He looked like all the life had been sucked clean from him. Hawthorn undid the rope and unlocked the shackles, then hauled the limp thief to his feet.

"Huh. He don't look near as grand up close compared to his wanted posters," Sheriff McGuire said.

"They rarely do," Hawthorn said.

V. The Sanctuary

The Garden of the Green Ladies lay just outside Gideonville's outskirts as McGuire said. It was a single structure carved out of white stone with grand arches, galleries, pavilions, colonnades, causeways and more stretching their length over a town sized piece of floating rock topped with luscious greenery: trees with glistening fruit and wild veins entwining their bodies like lazy snakes and emerald grasses that reached to a man's knee. A glistening waterfall, whose supply seemed somehow endless, spilled over the far side of the isle, its waters iridescent and crystalline like a million icy gems. Grand masses of ivy and flowers crowned the building's tops and bridges, some planted in immaculate hanging pots and baskets. A fuzzy, lavender colored mist cascaded from the garden's cliffs like an airy downpour of rainfall, bringing with it an aroma that was so powerful in its refreshing and soothing effects it nearly chased away the dust and dryness of the air around Gideonville. Almost.

The anchor, which looked to be made of metallic turquoise, dug itself hard and fast in the dirt, marking the beginning of the procession made of men and women that ran all the way up the garden's ivory steps. Hawthorn observed the customers. All were finely dress, prim and pristine, the women in flowing dresses of fine fabric and feathery lace, the men in suites and jackets with pin-stipes and gold embroidery. Politicians, businessmen, merchants, all well to do. *Standard clientele for the Green Ladies.*

Hawthorn lit himself a new cigarette and joined the line. He wasn't in the mood for waiting. He cut through the line as fast as possible, eliciting protests from the men and women alike. One yahoo even had the right amount of stupidity to step in the bounty hunter's way.

"Hey there! No cutting!"

Just a glare from Hawthorn's wicked eyes sent the man shaking back to his spot.

Hawthorn reached the foot of the steps where two of the Green Ladies stood. Both were tall and impossibly beautiful, dressed in long green gowns that almost covered the tips of their bare, pretty feet and left their shoulders exposed. The gowns themselves were made of leaves and thick woven vines, with flowers dotting the hems. One of the ladies had blonde hair that shimmered like gold, and eyes colored a burning emerald. The other had hair as black as a raven's feathers, irises that sparkled a luxurious, Springtime blue. They stopped their shouting of promises for treatments that would restore youth, fragrances that chased away nightmares, and balms to heal any and all kinds of pain to greet him.

"I am Isolde," said the blonde.

"And I am Morgan," said the raven haired.

"Welcome to our Gardens!" they said together.

"Morning. I want to see Headmistress Lillian."

The blonde gave him a masking smile. "The Headmistress is busy with other affairs. If you have questions regarding any of our salts, potions, tonics, lotions, ointments, oils, herbs, or salves, please feel free—"

"I came to see the Headmistress. Tell her it's Hawthorn."

The woman named Morgan broke in. "Good sir, if you would please exercise some patience and return to the line—"

"Tell her," he said, glaring at them both.

The girls hesitated, but the fluent, angelic sound of harp strings suddenly cut

off whatever they were going to say.

The two girls looked at each other, then at Hawthorn. "We will take you to the sanctuary," Isolde said.

VI. Lady Lillian

The sanctuary was much the same as when Hawthorn last set foot in its marble halls. Same vines, same flowers, same feeling of perpetual otherworldliness. It would've made Hawthorn feel like he had left the Wilds and gone halfway to Heaven. But he knew better.

The Ladies were leading the crowds in two different directions. The group going to the right, being led by a Lady named Diana, where headed to where all the beauty products and spa baths were. The other group, led by a Green Lady named Ophelia were being led off to the left. This group was mostly men.

The blonde, Isolde, took him down a separate corridor to a set of gold-inlaid alabaster steps. They went up the stairs and stopped at a pair of grand white stone doors. Isolde knocked.

"Headmistress," the Lady said.

"Yes?" The voice was patient and whimsically musical.

"I have the man with me. Mister Hawthorn."

"Let him enter."

The doors opened, and Hawthorn stepped in. They closed behind him, leaving Isolde out.

"You know, Hawthorn, it would be so much easier to call you by your first name," said the Headmistress. Lady Lillian left her mirror and flashed her dazzling green eyes at the bounty hunter. Her hair, a deep, luscious crimson with a hint of fire in it, fell down her bare shoulders in flowing curls. Her heart melting smile gleamed at him, emanating the same light that shined off her perfect skin.

Hawthorn lit a cigarette. "Ain't going to happen."

She kept her smile. "Ah, too bad." She decreased the distance between them and kept her gaze level with his, like a proud statue. "So, what brings the infamous bounty hunter, The Man That Never Sleeps, The Brute Killer, to my abode?" Her hand pressed against his rib, and slowly made its way over his midsection.

"That favor you promised me the last time our paths crossed."

"Ah," Her smile only gained magnitude. "I've been looking forward to this."

"I'm sure you have."

Her hand reached his belt buckle, then went slowly, agonizingly slowly, lower.

"And how can I fulfill it?" she said, her mouth just centimeters from his. He felt her warm breath on his face, her throat and neck craning.

"I need some medicine for my knee."

Her hand left him. "Medicine? You decided that you'd have me repay my debt by giving you...medicine?"

"It hurts real bad."

She crossed her arms and chuckled. "I must say. I was hoping for something a little more...enthralling."

"Sorry to disappoint."

"No, you're not."

She went to her massive cabinet. With a flick of a finger, the creamy oak piece of furniture opened to reveal shelf upon shelf of vials, bottles, and jars filled with liquids and creams colored every shade of the rainbow and beyond. She pulled one from the top shelf and handed it over to the bounty hunter.

"Obliged."

"You're welcome. Does that settle the debt?"

"Not quite."

She raised an eyebrow.

Hawthorn shrugged. "Hey, considering I risked my hide to save your skin while this glorified whorehouse of yours was on fire and threatening to fall on my head, I think I've earned the liberty to milk this debt situation for a little longer."

She gasped. "I resent that. It's not a whorehouse. Never once have my girls solicited their bodies for anyone's consumption or use in my halls."

Hawthorn smirked. "Right. Key words being 'in my halls.'"

Lillian flicked her hand in dismission. "It is true we explore the realms of pleasure here, but never illicitly or salaciously. And what we do, we do for more than monetary gain. My Ladies and I are of the belief that the body, though our vessel through this life it is, grows weary and rusty with time and worry. That being so, we provide services and products here that help to either stifle or lessen the effects," she said as she sat and checked her complexion in her silver-framed mirror. She stood and then went to a nearby vault, filigreed with designs of golden vines and crimson leafing. She flicked her finger again and the handled spun on command, the vault door swinging open. Inside were an assortment of ingredients and herbs sealed inside airtight glass tubing and vials. The ingredients themselves varied from plants colored all sorts of strange shades while emitting dim ethereal light to find powders that glimmered like pixie dust. Lillian took a white cylinder made of porcelain and decorated with winding green vines.

"We call it 'Opalescence.'"

Hawthorn took it in his hand. "Let me guess, it helps us 'discard' our human

vessels, like you said."

"Exactly. It allows the mind to separate from the body and experience a vast and unexplored array of sensations, transcending the limited prospects of our senses in their current state."

"Hm. Bottled euphoria."

She laughed a bit. "Bottled Euphoria, I like it, but it doesn't quite grow the garden I want."

Hawthorn gave the bottle back to her. "And in the midst of all this 'transcendence', you pocket a pretty little penny for it."

"Well, yes. The ingredients aren't exactly easy to acquire. But as I mentioned before, it's for a noble cause."

Hawthorn laughed. "Such a noble cause, without a doubt. And what about the side business? The one that includes spreading your wings as a soiled dove. I've heard the talk in the barrelhouses of the towns you've left. Men boast of having goddesses visit them in the night, entangling them in passion for a high fee, only to have them vanish like mist in the morn, leaving them lovelorn and sighing and aching."

Lillian went back to the mirror and kept her face straight in its reflection, occasionally snapping her finger, which then caused the mirror's surface to ripple as if a stone had been skipped across its surface. The mirror would then enlarge its image of her, allowing her to check every pore and crease in her skin. "What my girls do outside my halls, if those *are* my girls you're associates are gossiping about and not just stories meant to work as the inch marks on the measuring stick for comparing dick length, is their business."

"I reckon that applies to you too," Hawthorn said.

She stood and came close to him, letting her hands brush down his side to his hips. She gripped his belt and tugged; her red lips close to his chin. "Of course, it does."

Hawthorn took the cigarette from his mouth. "You ever get sick of trying?"

She let go of his belt with a bat of her eyes and returned to her seat. "What can I say, you're an exotic specimen. And the only man to ever tell me 'no'. Now you answer one of my questions: why do you need heeling salve? Got shot in the chase? Stabbed in a sabre duel?"

"I fell off my horse."

"I was being serious."

"So was I. Which reminds me, I could use some of that sleeping potion that ya'll carry."

"Which one?"

"The one that'll knock a man out for a week."

"What? Is the Man That Never Sleeps having bad dreams?"

"Kind of."

She went to her cabinet and pulled out another vial. She gave it to him, sighing. "Oh, Hawthorn. It would be nice if you could think of other, more pleasurable ways for me to make up the debt. It could be an adventure."

Hawthorn stuffed the potions into his satchel. "I've had enough adventures to last a few lifetimes."

She made a pouty face. "Well, at least let me show you around so you can see what I've done since I rebuilt the place. After all, I wouldn't have been able to

continue my business without your daring rescue."

Hawthorn decided to humor her. Best not to upset the hostess too much. "Alright."

She led him down the stairs and to the halls. Vines wrapped the pillars, their verdant limbs adorned with flower buds. The halls themselves were immaculate, with intricate designs carved into the roof and the tops of the pillars portraying plants and animals. Elaborately vivid friezes depicted scenes of nature, war, and love. Cowboys fighting the Ankari. Buffalo roaming the planes, and more.

"What do you think, so far?" Lillian asked.

"It definitely looks better when it ain't charred black."

"I'm so flattered by your artistic eye."

They reached the bathrooms. The steam was thick and warm, covering everything in a moist haze. An aroma, whose power was somewhere between strong and overwhelming, washed over Hawthorn's body as he came in. It smelled of honey and lavender mixed with some spice he could not pinpoint. Men preoccupied the baths, while the green gowned women massaged their backs and shoulders or fed them fruits on silver platters. They talked about trends in the mercantile realms with the Old World, Travis politics, stock prices for cattle, recent raids on the Gravesend Trail, along with art, music, and other high-brow prattle. He saw several of the maids poring bottles of Opalescence into the baths. The honeyed aroma emanated from those pools. The men in them wore looks saying they were flying free and high over hazy mountaintops, their eyes like wide and white dinner plates or blissfully closed as their heads rested on the side, inane grins spread across their slack-muscled faces like the lazy brushstroke of a mediocre painter, obscuring their visages, disfiguring them,

while the maids whispered in their ears and caressed and massaged their necks, temples, shoulders.

"See? As legitimate as can be," said Lillian beside him.

Hawthorn grunted his disbelief.

"Perhaps you would like to take a dip in the Opalescence? Loose yourself a bit,"

"No thanks. I like my mind where it is."

Then he heard shouting. One of the customers had gotten hold one of the girls. The girl was protesting, trying to kick him off. The man wasn't having it. And he had a gleam in his eyes Hawthorn had seen before. The bounty hunter drew one of his pistols when, suddenly, one of Lillian's gigantic vines came reaching through

one of the grand windows. The violator screamed as the vine wrapped around his waist and yanked him high into the air. All his flailing made him look like a rag doll gone maniacal. Hawthorn watched with mesmerized interest as the vine tossed the man out of the window. His high and helpless scream faded into the distance.

"I see the Sanctuary's still got a good ear." Hawthorn said, watching the rag doll man disappear.

"Oh, yes. No one harms my girls under my eyes. Or the Sanctuary's."

"You made that clear. You're not worried someone'll come looking for him?"

"I doubt anyone wants to scrutinize a floating island with lethal flora."

"Isn't that what you said last time?"

She dismissed his question with a wave of her hand. "I have it handled. Now, back to our talk..."

Suddenly Lillian was behind him, her arms wrapped around his waist. Her chest was pressed against his back; he felt her breasts through his shirt. She spoke in his ear. Her voice was mesmerizingly clear and mellifluous, yet hypnotically deep and sensual, with every movement of sound in her throat forming an enchantment that flittered delicately from the very tip her tongue. It beckoned, like a siren song, promising immense pleasure and ultimate satisfaction to every lust-filled fantasy a man's mind could conjure. So alluring and absorbing, like the sweetest and most spellbinding of melodies, it would make any man's worries instantly lift from his shoulders, only to replace any thought of pain or guilt with mad and insatiable desire, thus enslaving him to her will.

"Come and take me into your embrace, hunter. Make me feel your hard

body. I will give you my warmth. Take comfort in me, and I will soothe the pains from your flesh, cure the sufferings of your mind, and remove the sorrows in your heart." Every word had come smooth and lyrical, infused with delicate and enriching enticement. Hawthorn felt a rush of cold heat wash over the whole of his body, stinging his skin like needles, yet thrumming with a deep and quick pulse of erotic desire. He felt loose and unburdened, the weight coming off his back and falling to the floor in velvety sheets. He was relaxed, and he felt he could trust the welcome in her words, and that he could throw himself into her arms and he'd never want anything else again. Her voice went darker and sultrier in its tones; like the yearnful growls of a female panther at night. "Drink and be drunk on me," she said, a faint but enthralling groan ending each syllable.

Those last words would have been the final push for any other man, make him melt like butter beneath the desert sun right into Lillian's pretty hands. But

Hawthorn went as rigid and solid as stone at their sound. He spoke. "Last time I got drunk on something, I ended up in a fight with ten other men. By the time I came to my senses, nine of them were dead, and the tenth wished he were."

Softly, but firmly, he took her hands from his waist. He took a long drag from his cigarette, looked her in her astonished and disappointed face, then walked down the hall, same as he had entered it.

VII. Unwell Met

"You're a savage, Hawthorn! A brutal, heartless, damned savage!"

"Been called worse," Hawthorn said. "besides, you got a bath, didn't you?"

Dance went on raving behind the iron bars for another five minutes before finally settling. "The nerve of you, making me cross that plain on my bare feet."

"It's what you get for killing my horse." Hawthorn said.

"I killed...? You're the one who blew that creature's bloody brains out!"

"Because you went and fed it locoweed." Hawthorn leaned forward and grabbed the iron bars. The ruby eyes of the snakes seemed to glow, and the fang in his ear was made sharper by the candlelight. "Look here, Dance. I ain't as much a fan of this situation as you think. You've caused me enough trouble already. If you want to stay alive 'til we get to Redemption, then you'd better start staying in line. Unless you want to catch the likes of Gordy's Gang again."

Dance crossed his arms and sat down on his cot. "Staying alive. What makes you think they'll let me live when I get to Redemption?"

"I don't know. Not my job to know. I just handle the delivery."

Dance chuckled. "You're nothing but a slave Hawthorn. To money. To greed. Just another snake in the dust."

Hawthorn growled. "Listen Dance. you want to make something with the last weeks you have to spend on this good earth, then you'll listen and you'll listen straight. Only way I'm going to guarantee you get to Redemption safely is if I have an incentive. And I won't have that if you keep trying to escape. Now, come morning' we're leaving Gideonville, and you're takin' me to wherever you hid what you pilfered from Redemption. And this time they'll be no tricks, or the next thing that gets a bullet in its skull won't be a horse. Remember, I can still collect that prize with just your head in a sack. Savvy?"

Dance was too tired to argue any further, his rage having sapped what was left of his energy. He slumped to his cot and groaned. A moment later he breathed slowly. He was asleep. Hawthorn chuckled to himself. He'd get what he wanted from the thief in the morning. In the meantime, he needed to be alone with his own head.

The sheriff was snoring at his desk. Hawthorn decided to leave the two of them in their respective slumbers. He donned his hat and walked across the street to the Meriwether Saloon. He got to the swinging doors where his ears were filled with the usual shouts for rotgut and laments of bad card hands. Hawthorn took out his cigarette and killed it on the plank steps. He went inside.

Dealers were working hard and fast at shuffling cards while the players downed their whiskey and filled the air with tobacco smoke. The automaton bar tender, all prim and proper in his red and white striped apron and derby hat, nodded to Hawthorn as he took his seat at the table.

"What'll it be?" the automaton said in its pre-programmed drawl, its glass plated electric-blue optic ports looking blandly at him.

"A shot of Jack's Nine," Hawthorn said, pointing to a tall bottle with the signature black and white label. The automaton's wrist extended with a whir and he took the bottle from the shelf. He got a glass, quick as wind, and poured the hard drink all in one move.

Hawthorn put his money down. "Obliged."

The automaton tipped his hat and took the money, then went back to wiping the bar. Hawthorn took the shot in one gulp. He let it burn as he thought of

the road ahead. Next town on the map was Chancellorsville, and from there it would be about a week's ride to Redemption. He growled inwardly. That was a lot of time to put up with Dance. Even more, it was a long time to be out in the Wilds with such a big prize as the thief was.

Sooner than later, the stench of what went down in the Golden Times would get in the wind. And he could think of plenty of hounds who'd leap at the scent.

Jericho James, that Gavrokan upstart Revik, Jorhan "The Baron" von Skade, Webley, Broker, that rainbow haired, loud dressed yahoo Micky Merry, Stroke, Montcalm, and a whole host of others. All good, all ruthless. And all competition. They'd catch the tracks of his trail soon if they hadn't already. He called for another shot. *Yeah. It's going to be a long ride.*

The bartender, clicking and shifting as it did, poured him another. Hawthorn downed it again and was just about to ask concerning lodging when the yelling from one table got a little louder than the rest. Hawthorn turned around.

A group of soldiers, cavalrymen by the long, gold-lined red bands along their grey uniforms, were howling and cussing the way soldiers do when they'd too much whiskey.

Hawthorn tried to speak over them when one of the saloon girls came over to the soldier's table with a tray of fresh cooked steak. She had just finished putting the plates down when one of the soldiers, a good-for-nothing lieutenant, young and arrogant, grabbed the girl's backside. "Hold on there!"

The girl grunted as the lieutenant hauled and pinned to her his lap. "Come on, lassie! Show us a little good time!" Then he forced her to bend over on his knees, drew up her skirt, and swatted her hard on her petticoats. The woman yelped and

started crying. The soldiers laughed.

Hawthorn grumbled. "Leave the bottle." The bartender did so. Hawthorn took the Jack's Nine in his hand and got up from the bar. He approached the soldier's table and stood behind them.

"Such respectable conduct for soldiers," he growled.

The soldiers just kept laughing. The lieutenant arched backward in his chair, guffawing all the way. "Damned be respectable conduct! We've been in this mudhole now for a month, and all the whores and whiskey is starting to taste stale! Besides, what business is it to you, Mister—?"

"Hawthorn."

The other soldiers stopped laughing and looked at him, their eyes slowly widening and their skin growing paler once they realized who it was talking to them.

The lieutenant stopped laughing and wiped his face of its tears. "Hawthorn. Well, Mister Hawthorn you can just go and—"

"Uh, sir," one of the soldiers said, pulling on his superior's sleeve.

"What, now, Jameson?"

Jameson pointed. Suddenly, the lieutenant could see. He bolted upward and let the lady go. She wailed and whimpered as she hurried up the saloon steps.

The lieutenant couldn't find words to fit his drunk tongue for a moment. "Hawthorn. Certainly, not *the* Hawthorn."

"Certainly so."

The other soldiers got up and made distance.

Hawthorn stepped up to the lieutenant and got right in his face. "I think you owe that lady there an apology."

The lieutenant decided to straighten his spine and lift his chin. "And I say I don't Mister Hawthorn."

Hawthorn heard it then. The soft slide of metal against leather, the subtle click of a gun's hammer.

"You'd better do it, boy," Hawthorn said.

The gun was out of its holster now.

"And what'll happen if I—"

Hawthorn smashed the bottle across the lieutenant's face, and in the same motion drew his left pistol, spun, and fired. Jameson, the one who'd drawn his own gun, went to the saloon's floor with a howl, his gun-hand all bloody. The lieutenant, meanwhile, went crashing into the game table and onto the floor, dragging the table, cards, chips, and glasses all with him.

"That's what'll happen," Hawthorn growled. He looked at the bottle. "And such a waste of a good whiskey."

All the laughter and music died. Everyone's attention went to Hawthorn and the soldiers.

The others were angry now. The last two of the soldiers charged him. Hawthorn sidestepped one of them, let a bit of his foot out, and sent the soldier sprawling to the floor. The other took a swing at Hawthorn's face. Hawthorn swept it aside and brought his own fist right under the soldier's jaw. He went to the floor and didn't get up. He heard the last soldier's running footfalls coming up behind him.

Hawthorn sidestepped again, swung his fist out and caught the soldier in the neck. The soldier flipped backward and crashed back-first to the floor. Before he could get up, Hawthorn finished him with a kick across the face.

Hawthorn turned around. The lieutenant was on his feet again, with a gun in his hand. Shaking, he aimed it at Hawthorn. The lower half of his face was covered in blood from the jagged cut put there by the Jack's Nine bottle.

"I'm going to...kill you..."

Hawthorn was annoyed. "Put it down, boy."

The lieutenant kept aiming the gun, his finger beginning to squeeze the trigger. Hawthorn could feel everyone's eyes on them. Even the automaton's. Hawthorn stepped closer to the bleeding soldier.

"Put it down," Hawthorn said.

The lieutenant stared Hawthorn in his red and green eyes, holding the gaze for a straight second before his finger stopped squeezing the trigger. The lieutenant let the gun clatter to the floor.

"Atta boy." Hawthorn went over and yanked the boy lieutenant to his feet. He then slammed officer against the bar-top, shattering a couple shot glasses in the process. The boy looked at him, eyes-wide and still foggy from the liquor, but still fearful.

"Next time I see or hear you mistreating a lady while I'm still in town, I won't go so easy on you. You hear me, greenhorn?"

"Y-yes, sir."

"Good."

A gunshot cracked the air. Hawthorn turned to see Sheriff McGuire standing with his gun aimed at the ceiling, its barrel smoking. Next to him stood a tall soldier with the eagle and star of a colonel on his feathered hat, all neat and pretty in his uniform. Four more armed soldiers flanked them, all armed with rifles.

"That's enough, bounty hunter."

Hawthorn gave the lieutenant one last glare and let him go. The lieutenant scrambled to the colonel's side where the two started talking. A moment passed before the lieutenant left the colonel's presence to collect his fallen and beaten buddies. Together, they all limped out the door.

McGuire spoke. "Dang damn it, Hawthorn. What were you doing in here fighting these fellas?"

"They were getting on my nerves."

McGuire spoke again. "And that justifies you putting bullets in them?"

Hawthorn rolled another cigarette. "Be glad I didn't kill them."

The colonel stepped over to Hawthorn. His hair, long and obscenely blond, was flowing down in graciously perfect curls and his long golden mustache drooped down his chin. In every way, he looked the epitome of the Romantic and legendary rider and soldier so popularized, Hawthorn had seen, back East in the papers and tabloids. But Hawthorn knew better.

The colonel shook his head as he walked over to Hawthorn, golden tresses swinging back and forth over his face like a rag doll. His gloved hands behind his back, the glare in his eyes burning with contempt as he looked down his nose at Hawthorn, despite that they were the same height.

"Pleasant to you make your acquaintance once again, Hawthorn," the colonel said, an audible bite in his every syllable.

Hawthorn stuck the cigarette between his teeth and drew a match to its tip before answering. "Can't say the same for you, Gordonson."

Gordonson started coughing a little from the smoke. He wiped his mouth
and scowled.

"How's the shoulder?" Hawthorn said.

"Not bad, since you shot it. You have any idea how much you embarrassed me that day?"

"Don't feel too bad. It was a bit embarrassing for me too, especially since I much rather would have shot you in the head."

The scowl deepened. "I didn't come here to toss shit back and forth with you, Hawthorn."

"That so?"

"You've hurt—hell—nearly *killed* my men today."

"Sure did."

"You're going to answer for it."

"Uh-huh."

Gordonson slammed his boot to the planks. "I won't tolerate this disrespect from you, bounty hunter!"

Hawthorn couldn't be more disinterested in the colonel's threats. That didn't stop the colonel's cotton-puffed face from turning a seething shade of red.

"Damn you, Hawthorn! I won't accept this arrogance! You attacked and viciously maimed uniformed soldiers of the Republic!"

Hawthorn's voice raised to a menacing growl. "Yeah. For abusing an innocent girl who did nothing but serve them steak."

"Enough!"

Gordonson turned to McGuire. "I want this man in irons! My men will escort him to the fort's brig, where he'll stay until this matter is settled." He gestured for the soldiers to come forward.

McGuire nodded obediently, if not a little disappointedly. He walked up to Hawthorn with a set of shackles, his posture tense, like he expected Hawthorn to make a move.

"Your weapons," the sheriff said.

Hawthorn looked from McGuire to Gordonson to the other soldiers to all the people still left in the saloon. His hands went to his guns. The soldiers brought their rifles to bear. He looked all four of them in the eyes. They were young, all of them. Young and nervous. He could see the shakiness in their eyes, their hands, their mouths, the sweat beading on their brows. They knew he was, knew what he could do with a gun and his hands. He briefly wondered if they had any family, any wives and kids, or were they still getting drunk and chasing hookers when they got the chance. Whatever. He could've killed them all, right then and there. But that would've been against his better judgment. Still, he could've done it.

He took out his pistols, turned them around in his hands, and handed them over to the sheriff by the barrels. The sheriff took the guns. Hawthorn gave over his knife too. One of the soldiers took that. McGuire proceeded to fasten and lock the shackles on Hawthorn's wrists.

"There," McGuire said. Then he looked up and whispered to Hawthorn. "You ain't going to kill me after this all over, are you?"

Hawthorn smirked while his eyes sparkled. "Nah," he whispered back.

"Get him out of here!" hollered Gordonson.

The four soldiers ushered Hawthorn out by the barrels of their rifles.

VIII. Sentenced to Sacrifice

Hawthorn said nothing as the iron bars were slammed shut, sealing both he and Dance in Fort Greer's cells.

"Sorry it had to come to this, Hawthorn," McGuire said.

The bounty hunter shrugged. "Just another turning of the sun," Hawthorn said.

"Yes. Another turn that will end up with you hanging from a noose," The scarred lieutenant, named Bannister, said. The colonel had let him accompany the group to the cells in an attempt to pacify his damaged ego.

"Huh. And here I am thinking I was innocent until proven guilty,"

That made the young officer reach for his cavalry sabre.

Gordonson grabbed him by the wrist. "Control yourself, boy!" The lieutenant looked at the colonel, then nodded slowly.

The colonel released him and looked back at Hawthorn. "Before a decision can be reached concerning your sentence, Hawthorn, you will be confined here until further notice and kept under guard at all times. Same goes for Mister Dance."

"Whatever," Hawthorn said.

"Don't I get a say here?" Dance pleaded.

Gordonson ignored him. The two soldiers left to lead McGuire out of the fort.

"So, what to say what to say," Dance said to Hawthorn through the wall separating their cells.

Hawthorn growled.

"I just find it interesting how fate plays with twists and turns. There you

were standing on the other side of my cell back in town, and, in less than an hour's time, here we both are in the same situation! I thought bounty hunters were supposed to stay on the right side of the law."

Hawthorn hocked a wad of spit onto the ground at the foot of his cell. "These bastards ain't the law. They're everything the law's against." He glanced at the thief. "Your kind of people, Dance."

The thief chuckled scornfully. "They hardly seem like *my* kind of people."

Hawthorn growled and leaned against the railing. Just then he heard footsteps approaching.

Lieutenant Bannister came back a moment later with five men. They opened the cell.

"Step out," the lieutenant said, an arrogant smile creeping up the corner of his lip.

Hawthorn had a feeling he wouldn't like where this would take him. And he still felt the same way after he'd been struck in the nose, back, and stomach with rifle stocks. He collapsed to his knees as blood trailed down from his nose and over his lip.

He glared up at the lieutenant, who then finished him with a strike to the temple.

IX. The Argentavis

The smell of open air was the first thing he awoke to. That, and the sound of rushing water.

He was in a cage, just barely big enough to allow him sitting space. He blinked and his eyes cleared. He first found that his guns and knife were missing. No surprise there. His eyes then went to his cage.

The cage was made of faded, rotting wood that made both the bottom and top. Black cords connected the thing to the bars that held him in. Bars that, as Hawthorn looked closer, were made of bone. Hawthorn crawled forward as much as he could.

The cage itself was suspended by a cracked and scraggly rope over a narrow gorge that yawned deeply below him. Several other cages, some intact, but most ripped and mauled to absolute shreds, also dangled from the rope. He could make out the river, its foaming waters storming in white masses. Above him, casting a narrow shadow, was singular mesa peak that resembled a sharp needle.

Hawthorn knew where he was now.

"Enjoying the view?"

Hawthorn looked up at the cliff-side. Gordonson was standing there with about a dozen more men.

Hawthorn cursed the colonel under his breath. "Yeah. Why don't you come down here and join me? I saved a spot for you under my boot here."

Gordonson laughed. "Always the clever one, Hawthorn. But in this case that sharp mouth of yours finally bit off more than it could chew." The colonel pointed a gloved finger to the peak ahead.

"With a knowledge of the Wilds as prolific as yours, Brute Killer, I expect you know what that peak is over yonder?"

"I do," Hawthorn growled.

He spoke with his hands on his hips, his chest puffing out like a rooster's. "Then I hope you feel honored. The Neotok think of the mighty Argentavis as a god. Before we drove them from this cursed strip of barren earth, they'd take prisoners, slaves, hell, even their own chief's kids and leave him here in these cages to be fed to that monster. They thought the thing was the guardian of the river, and by sacrificing to him they'd ensure a most bountiful harvest."

"Funny, I never took you for a man of religion, Gordonson," Hawthorn said.

"Well, I am today, Hawthorn. I hope you enjoy becoming sanctified." He laughed, and his men joined him. They turned to walk away, but Gordonson stopped one final time. "Oh, and don't worry about that bounty on Dance's head. I'll be sure to make good on it. The Army could always use a few more spare funds, what with those policies swimming in the Senate now..." The colonel went to grumbling and walked away. Soon, he and the soldiers were gone.

They left him to the wind and water. Hawthorn looked down again at the rushing river, then at the jagged walls of dusty orange rock that flanked both his sides. The drop wouldn't kill him, but it sure would make him sore. And the cliffs. Maybe if he could break from the cage, he could shimmy across on the rope to the cliffs. But the rope looked on the point of busting already.

Hawthorn thought. One thing was for certain. If he didn't get out of the cage soon, that damned Agentavis would show...

Suddenly a horrid, sharp screech echoed across the gorge with the force of thunder. The sound grated its way through Hawthorn's ears, which made him clasp his hands as close to his head as possible. A dark shape had taken form high in the sky, streaking black across the sun's gold face. It flew far past the horizon, vanishing in the blue. At that distance, it had appeared no larger than the average eagle.

Hawthorn knew better.

He grabbed the bone bars of the cage and pulled. The bones were old, grimy and dusty, but still strong. He gritted his teeth, the teeth of his necklace jingling, the fang from his ear shaking, and the snake tattoos shining. He pulled, and pulled, straining his muscles. The cords were like iron.

He gave up with his hands.

"Alright," he gasped. He decided to try another approach. He scooted back as far in the box-like cag as his tall body would allow. He brought his legs in, and kicked. The bottoms of his black, snakeskin boots slammed hard against the bones, the spurs grating across the old wood.

Nothing. The bones still held. He cursed and tried again. Still nothing. He decided not to curse and tried again.

A crack. The bone splintered a bit. He uttered an excited laugh and kicked again. And again.

Two bars of the bone cage snapped, leaving sharp remains behind. It wasn't a hole big enough for him to crawl out of, and it had made the thing rock on the rope. Hawthorn crawled forward. He grabbed one of the bits of bone he'd broken, his strikes having reduced it to a sharp spike. He yanked it free from the cords. He took his positon again and was ready to kick. He looked at the sky.

No sign of the bird.

He sighed with relief. *Maybe the thing decided to eat something else's flesh.* He hoped it had. He kicked again, managing to snap another bar off and shake the thing mightily when a gust of wind suddenly slammed the cage, making it rock worse. Hawthorn grabbed the insides of the cage, thinking he heard something snap.

Then things darkened. A shadow passed over him, blotting out the sun completely and stretching over the cliffs, bleeding down their sides. For a sheer moment, everything was shrouded in that shadow. Then the light reached in again.

Hawthorn had gone still. Now, he crept up and peeked out the breach in the cage. The sky was clear and blue. Nothing.

He went back to his position.

Then a claw, as big as his arm, pierced the cage's top. Hawthorn went to his back, his legs pinned against the walls, boots up against the roof where the claw wasn't. Another claw wrapped around the cage's outside, covering every inch of opening. The cage had stopped rocking, held still by the big bird's grip. A foul stench descended like a cloud, burning Hawthorn's eyes.

Then an eye looked into the cage. It was blood red, the sclera white as bone, and the pupil black. A black point in white nothing, surrounded by pale, pinkish flesh.

Hawthorn gripped the bone shard tight.

Then the cage was torn. Shards of bone and wood clogged the air and exploded through the confined space. Hawthorn's vision went blurry, obscured by debris. Splinters scratched his arms and face in a storm of shrapnel. He covered his eyes. The cage's bottom gave out. He fell.

The world spun and cascaded around him, all going too fast in a whirling

blur. He caught sight of something coming at him. A big talon. It grabbed for his legs. Hawthorn, still in control of his freefall, twisted out of the talon's clutch just in time. Then he reached forward, a bit blindly, and caught onto the rearmost talon.

The Argentavis released its scream again.

Most would be able to tell why the Neotok thought of the bird as a god. It was easily the size of an engorged barn. Its tremendous wings nearly spanned the width of the canyon. Its feathers were blacker than night, and its ancient, vulture-like head was colored a bloody pink and covered with flaps of bulgy flesh that dangled from its neck and temples like sacks. It craned its long neck high into the sky and screeched again, its pale beak opened wide. Hawthorn briefly wondered how many carcasses had been consumed in its big belly. But only briefly.

He had the bone shard in his hand. He reached up and stabbed the shard into the giant bird's leg. The bird's flesh was a lot harder than he anticipated. But the bone shard stuck nonetheless. The Argentavis screeched, its body shuddered from the sudden prick.

He reached up with his free hand and clutched a tuft of feathers.

The Argentavis was getting violent now. Its long, pink and bald vulture head looked down at him. It started shaking its leg. Hawthorn held on for dear life. His head spun, his vision jostling as the Argentavis tried to shake him off, rattling his insides.

"Alright, you overgrown buzzard..."

He braced his boots against the bird's toes and launched himself up. He was under the bird's massive wing now, the wind whipping his hair. Hawthorn turned in time to see the big beak coming at him. Hawthorn let go of the feathers, making it

out of the way by the skin of his teeth. The beak with its rough and stinking surface grazed his face.

For a moment, Hawthorn was in free fall again. He quickly grabbed hold of the beak. The neck swung back, again trying to detach him. Hawthorn grunted, cursed. He was lying flat on his chest on top of the beak. The bird's white and red eyes stared him, big as ponds. He still had the bone shard.

The Argentavis opened its mouth for another screech. Again, the world went right on its end. Hawthorn gritted his teeth as the blood rushed to his head, then his face.

He was getting tired of this. He let go of the beak and let himself slide over the rough surface. The Argentavis's face rushed up to him. He got the bone shard ready. He came face to face with the bird's right eye. It glistened coldly like a still pond. He jabbed the bone right into it.

Now the bird really screamed.

Hawthorn stayed lodged on the beak, letting the gore from the pierced eye ooze over his arm. He dug the bone shard in as hard and far as he could. The Argentavis's giant head shook like a snake's rattler. Hawthorn was getting dizzy, but he held on.

The Argentavis's flight went wild. Hawthorn flattened himself against the bird's beak as much as possible to avoid being cut in half by a sharp cliff-edge. They struck something. Hawthorn's whole body jarred and shook.

"Damn!"

The bird had crashed into the side of the gorge with a harsh crack that echoed off the rocky walls. Its head snapped backed and a big gash had nearly rent its

skull in two. The bird fell. The water rushed up to them, its roaring filling all space. Hawthorn let go of the shard and fell with the Argentavis.

He slammed into the water. The impact stunned him for a moment, along with the sudden burst of cool water soaking him to the skin. The Argentavis crashed at the same time. Its impact sent a pluming explosion of glittering water high into the air, along with an instant tidal wave that sent Hawthorn hurtling down the river. He rolled and spun under the water like a barrel of apples, trying hard to keep water from flooding his lungs. Things went by at blurring speed. He finally managed to break the river's foamy surface and catch a breath. He choked and sputtered.

He turned around to see the Argentavis's body coming fast at him. He took a quick breath and dove again, narrowly missing one of its limp wings sweeping him up. The water went dark as night as the enormous carcass tumbled over him with a muffled rumble. As soon as the sun shone through the water again, he dove upward.

He was out of the gorge. Hilly, rocky land appeared around him. He made a course for the sandy bank. A lone dogwood stood there, its branches groping out over the water from between some rocks. Hawthorn, struggling against the current, grabbed hold of a branch from the crooked tree. He hauled himself onto the bank, then fell on his back into the soft dirt. He drank the air.

He turned his face and looked at the glittering waters in the noon sun. The Argentavis's dead body rolled on by, carried by the water like the hands that carried a corpse to its coffin. There was something almost peaceful in it. Grotesquely peaceful. He sighed and looked away, thinking about how he had just killed a god.

X. The Voice

"Any sign of the bird?" Lieutenant Bannister asked.

Private Smithers was the first to answer. "No, sir. I thought I saw something streaking across the sky a moment ago, but I took it for a trick of the eye."

"We haven't heard a damn thing since that last cry," said Sergeant Perkins. "It went diving into the gorge and it hasn't come back."

"You don't think he killed it, do you?" Asked Corporal Polanski.

"What? You got a walnut for a brain? Did you see how big that thing was? No wonder those cursed Ankari worshiped it!"

"Yeah, I did see it. I also noticed that the sky is blue today. I'm just saying I've heard some things about that Hawthorn fella. None of it pretty, all of it scary."

Bannister thought to himself as he sat on the rock overlooking the gorge. The possibility of that heterochromatic, simple-minded, dirt-eating bumpkin who thought himself as something just because of his guns managing to kill the Argentavis...It was too much to digest. No. No, it was impossible.

And yet here they were, guarding the only path from the gorge that led back to Gideonville.

He fingered the trigger of his lever action. He'd let a few more minutes pass, then he'd send half of the dozen men posted with him to go check. Perkins would lead them. He was a trustworthy man. The rest of the soldiers all thought Hawthorn had been caught helping the Neotok raid on Gideonville and a few other nearby towns, which meant he was partly responsible for all the land burnings, rapes, and massacres the savages had perpetrated over the last month. So, the soldiers didn't mind if they could have a little fun with the mongrel before he went on his

jolly way to Hell. Only Bannister, the colonel, and a few select NCOs, like Perkins, knew better.

"Sergeant Perkins, take a few men and—"

"Uh, sir—" said Private Stallworth.

"Damn it, Stallworth! I'm giving an order!"

"You might want to take a look at this."

The private was looking through his spyglass. The lieutenant left his position and stomped over to the private.

"What is it?"

The private handed him the telescope without saying a word. He just stared far ahead.

The lieutenant put the spyglass to his eyes. And his heart rammed into his throat.

He saw the Argentavis, floating gently down the river's current, its enormous body nearly consuming the entirety of the river. Its ugly, pink and mangled head bent backward at an odd angle, bright blood oozing from its wounds, and its eyes, pale and glassy, staring emptily at the sky.

Bannister took the spyglass from his eye once it drifted into range of his normal sight. He could feel the eyes of his men looking past his shoulders and at the dead Neotok god themselves. It drifted on past them, following the glistening waters.

"Ah, shit..." said the sergeant.

Suddenly their gazing was cut off by a gunshot.

* * *

Hawthorn had seen their shapes coming up the rocky slope. About a dozen

soldiers, waiting to bushwhack him on the way up. But Hawthorn had taken it quietly. He'd even removed the spurs from his boot heels, but left one in his right hand.

Once the soldiers spotted the Argentavis's corpse floating downriver, their attention had been diverted. That gave Hawthorn the chance to get behind one of them. He wrapped his arm around the soldier's neck and drew his spur across the esophagus. Blood spurted out from the gash. He could feel the flow of life in the neck stop, the muscles go limp and slack as warm red poured over his wrist. As the body fell, Hawthorn's right hand went to the soldier's belt and pulled out his gun.

He drew, took aim, and fired. One went down. Now, he had their attention. The rest all turned to face him, but Hawthorn caught two more before they could draw a bead on him. He dove behind a cluster of rocks as the lead shower started.

Gunshot echoed all around, rebounding off the canyon sides like thundercracks. The bullets chipped the rock away.

Bannister pointed at the rock. "Pour it on!" His men obeyed, their fingers glued to their triggers. He then gave hand signals for Perkins to take five men and flank on the left, while he took the rest and flanked on the right.

We'll box him in tighter than a rat caught in a drum.

They carried out his orders. Perkins's men reached the rock first. He called out. "He ain't here!"

"What?!" Bannister said. He gave the order to cease fire before they gathered around the rock. Sure, enough, there was no sign of Hawthorn.

"Blast it! Where'd that damn snake get to!?" he turned his rage on his men, "Fan out! Find him! Kill him!" The lieutenant's face had gone so red the scar was starting to bleed through its stitches. The men did as they were told.

The rocks melded into a set of low hills. Hawthorn, while the volley of gunfire hammered the rock, had taken a narrow path between the rocks and gone further into the hills. He stood atop a low one and watched as the ten remaining soldiers split ranks and started roaming the rocks.

He smiled to himself. There were as good as dead now.

He climbed down the hill and went to work. He clambered down the rocks with all the grace of a fox, on his way to a group of three men that were heading up the west side of the hillsides. He took his place beneath the shadows of a tall rock. He passed into the darkness and waited for the three soldiers to go by.

They were quiet, searching every angle. Hawthorn quickly crossed the path, silent as a serpent, and went around to the other side. The soldiers were just a few feet in front of him. He took out the knife he liberated from the soldier he killed with the spurs. He got behind the rearmost soldier, and grabbed him by the neck, careful to cover his mouth as he did. Again, the warm blood spilled over his arm.

The other two had made it about a hundred feet before they realized he was gone.

"Uh, Sergeant?" said the private. "Where's Polanski?"

Perkins looked behind him. "Blast it," Rocks surrounded them on all sides. Too many shadows, too many small places.

"Keep your rifle up." he told the private. "We make for the high ground."

They climbed further up through the hills, finally reaching a steep outcropping. They took position on the cliff's edge. It gave them a bird's eye view on the paths and hills around them. They trained their rifles on the paths.

"Come on, you squirmy bastard, show those pretty eyes of yours," Perkins

said.

"Sure thing." Both soldiers turned around. The hunter stood over them, white hair bright, eyes shining like something out of the abyss, fierce green and murderous red. The teeth jingled in the wind.

The last thing the two soldiers saw were the barrels of Hawthorn's guns.

* * *

Bannister and the last six had gathered at the foot of a hill. They heard the echoing gunfire.

"What was that?" said Private Smithers.

"Hawthorn's killed another of us," said one of the more jaded soldiers.

"What makes you think it wasn't one of us who killed him?" said Private Reuter.

The soldier gave Reuter a scowl and gestured to the silence all around them. "If you had just killed *the* Hawthorn, would you keep quiet about it?"

Bannister turned on them both in harsh whispers. "Shut it, the both of you! Take position. If that snake's game is to pick us off one by one, then he'll have to do differently with us. We'll hold here and wait for him to come. He can't take all of us at once."

"From what I've heard—" began another private.

"Shut it! That's an order!"

They all took position. In clefts, behind the rocks, and on the hill slopes. All

angles of entrance were covered; all paths were watched. Bannister was confidant. *That white haired, pretty-eyed, godless scum of a bounty hunter doesn't have a chance—*

"There he is!"

All guns went to a figure standing on a hill overlooking their position, shrouded by the shadows of the midafternoon sun.

"Open fire!" Bannister yelled.

Fire leaped from the rifle barrels. The figure shook as the rounds tore through it. It jolted and quaked, bullets piercing its head, chest, legs, and arms. Finally, it fell to the ground.

"He didn't even fire back," someone said.

Bannister and a couple others left their cover to inspect the body. The first thing they noticed was that whoever they shot wasn't dressed like Hawthorn.

"Why is he wearing one of our uniforms?"

Bannister cursed and flipped the body over. "By Hell! It's Perkins!"

Suddenly, a cruel and wild laugh, saturated with the utmost and sublime inhumanity, touched their ears. All sharp chill stung them all at once.

Then it ceased.

"What was that?" the private next to Bannister said, just before a bullet split his head open. Blood splattered over Bannister's face. He reeled around right as another bullet smashed into his ribs, knocking him to the ground.

Another soldier hollered. He clutched his chest and rolled down the foot of the hill. He was followed by another, shot straight through the heart. Hawthorn appeared on top of the hill, and Bannister watched the bounty hunter, the air warping around his blazing guns. Bannister felt his wound, saw the blood straining

between his fingers. A hot and lurid pain like molten lead, thick and bulging, ravaged his chest until it stopped in his intestines where it burned at the Insides. Bright spots specked his vision. His mind become afloat in a steaming sea, blood pushing against

the seams in his face, his eyes, ready to burst. He was vaguely aware of his last few

men falling, their bodies hitting the earth then spilling out blood like they were cracked eggs as the hunter stood atop the rock with his blazing guns, the fire from the barrels warping the air, the scales of the snakes on his arms shimmering like breathing scales, the teeth on his neck and the fang from his ear making faint notes when brushed by the wind, like pale wind chimes.

His vision suddenly glazed, like he was looking through melting glass. The sunlight went prismatic as reality shimmered and shifted in the bounty hunter's wake. The gun-smoke that wavered around him rose, red and orange flame from barrel flashes intertwined with acrid grey and black, wrapping around his arms and legs, his chest and neck. The smoke and fire then were solid. The shape bended and curved; serpentine. A snake's head formed, fangs of black crystal encased flame, eyes jewels of shifting red and orange and yellow. The head rested on the hunter's shoulder and then stared directly at Bannister, its fiery tongue flicking.

Bannister clenched his eyes shut, sweat streaming over the eyelids as a pulsing burst of piercing white bleached the dark wall. Terror.

* * *

Hawthorn took the moment to leave his cover and get closer. He had just made the slope when the last soldier appeared from around the rock, a bayonet fixed to his rifle's barrel. The soldier hollered loud and charged. Hawthorn sidestepped, allowing the rifle to pass right by his arm. He grabbed the rifle as it passed with both

hands and pulled. Since he was at a lower elevation, he pulled down and kept his foot out. The soldier immediately lost balance, then tumbled down the hill after tripping over Hawthorn's foot.

He hit the earth with a low thud, face first. Before he could get up, Hawthorn leapt down and impaled the soldier in the back with his own rifle. The soldier screamed, made a gurgling noise, went still.

Hawthorn sighed and wiped his head of sweat. He heard panting.

The lieutenant was still alive, albeit by a thread. His face had turned a deathly pallid shade. With the smoothness of youth, he looked almost like a china doll on the verge of shattering. Blood seeped through the spaces between his fingers as he clutched his wounded side, his eyes shut tight like he was trying to fight off the pain.

Hawthorn stepped up to him. The lieutenant unshut his eyes, gasped, and started grabbing for his rifle which lied not but a couple inches beyond the reach of his fingertips. The muscles in his face were strained and contorted like a tugged rope. Hawthorn kicked the away.

The lieutenant looked up at him, eyes so wide and clear with terror Hawthorn saw his reflection in them; hair white as death, eyes mismatched, demonic, otherworldly. What he saw was a creature, a beast before him, with teeth on his body and snakes on his arms.

"You—you killed me...You killed all of them." The lieutenant looked past his wounds to the corpses of his men.

Hawthorn said nothing. He just looked down at the dying man.

Bannister, gasping, met Hawthorn's mismatched eyes. "What—what kind of man are you?"

Hawthorn knelt to the lieutenant's face. "What kind of man am I?"

He grabbed the back of Bannister's neck, propped up his head, then shoved his gun, barrel first, into the lieutenant's mouth. Bannister choked, the taste of metal

and gun-smoke mingling with the blood in his mouth. Hawthorn shoved it back so far, Bannister convulsed with gagging heaves. Hawthorn held it there.

And he spoke. "I once got in a fight with ten other men in a saloon. Nine of them I killed. Quick and simple. But the last...first I cut out his eyes with a fork, then I shoved them both down his throat. I did the same with his balls. And I did that while I was DRUNK!"

He got in the lieutenant's face, shoving the gun in farther. The lieutenant's eyes were sad now, and watery.

"That's the kind of man I am, boy. And you want know something about what kind of man you are?"

Bannister whimpered. Snot drained from his nose as he started crying and choking.

Hawthorn spoke low. "You're nothing."

He fired. Half the lieutenant's head was blown out the back. Hawthorn let what was left slump to the ground.

Hawthorn got to his feet. A tune entered his head. He walked away, whistling "Sam Hall".

And the notes carried over the wind.

XI. The Debt Paid

The moonlight gleamed from the walls of Green Ladies' sanctuary. It seemed almost heavenly, sublimely serene. It even glittered, and the lavender mist had turned a soft, effulgent blue.

The steps were gone. By the morning the whole thing would have evanesced, gone to leech off another town. But he needed in, just one more time.

Hawthorn stood beneath the floating island's shadows. He knew that Lillian knew he was there. She could hear him breathing. She was like that. "A pining lover's senses are attuned to every move and breath of her desired" she said. Hawthorn had said nothing.

The steps revealed themselves for him. He climbed up to the Sanctuary's grand door, which also opened without any physical effort. He stepped inside and walked down the pale halls. They were empty, lifeless. Ghostlike. Blood dripped from his body, none of it his own, onto the white marble floors. He reached Lillian's chamber. They opened for him as well.

Lillian was lying sidewise on a lounging sofa, her body clothed in a night blue gown, her hair forming a perfect curtain of crimson curls over her fair shoulders. A vine, laced with supple, violet grapes that looked ready to burst at the slightest lick, dangled through a window, just within Lillian's reach. She daintily took a grape from the vine's verdant flesh and bit into it, the juice running down her lips.

She talked without looking at him. "Come to milk more from our little arrangement?"

"You could say that.", he said, with blood running down his neck.

"And how may I satisfy you this time?" Her tone had steadily lowered with a seductive diminuendo after every word.

"A bath would be good."

At this point she turned to look at him with smile that held but the faintest hint of a victory, but then she saw the blood.

"Oh." she said, simply. "You look dreadful."

"Thanks."

"None of its yours, I presume?"

"You've presumed right."

She finished her grape and got to her feet. The vine retreated through the window.

"We really must stop meeting like this."

"I really need that bath, and something else," Hawthorn said.

She made her fingers walk along Hawthorn's shoulder. "Oh?"

"It's going to cost you."

"I'm listening." her fingers reached the button of his shirt.

"I need you to...solicit your services to Gordonson and his officers for free, tonight."

She took her fingers away. "Excuse me?"

"Yeah."

She turned away from him, arms crossed, her the dark sapphire train of her gown trailing with her. "I thought we'd been over this. We're not a brothel."

"And I thought I'd made it clear that's horse-hockey, Lillian. You may say that whatever your girls do outside your little island is their business and all, but don't

tell me you've never known."

She spoke with her back to him. "I've...never encouraged it."

"But you allowed it, and it's all the same in my book. And despite all your claims of being a legitimate business, you've pocketed some of their earnings, like any proper madam would."

She spun on him then, green eyes aflame. "And so what if I have?" she shouted. Vines started snaking through the open window and the railing of the marble veranda, some coiling around Lillian's arms and others remaining motionless in the air, poised like vipers ready to strike.

Hawthorn stood his ground, eyes fixed on Lillian as she went on.

"You think we just reside up here like nymphs in a meadow, free from threat and danger. But, let me tell you, Hawthorn, that you have no idea what I've had to do to keep this place, my *home*, safe. Do have any conception, the tiniest inkling, of what kind of power lives in a place like this, and how many cutthroats and blackguards would do anything to get their hands on it? An island that floats, Hawthorn! So yes, perhaps I've allowed my girls to offer themselves as payment for debts owed so that my sanctuary remains unmolested, and maybe some of them pursued their own ventures. But I made sure that whatever they did or had to do, it was never free, though maybe at a reduced price."

"Lillian, he's got something in that fort of his that belongs to me. And it would be a lot easier for me to get it if his eyes were focused on something else. Along with the rest of his body."

She got in his face, the vines spreading from her arms like tentacles. Hawthorn didn't flinch as they wrapped around his legs and arms, snugly but not

painfully. *Yet.* "Have you not heard a word I just said? This debt I owe doesn't grant you control over me and my business to where I and it bark and fetch like a dog, bounty hunter. You can't just—"

"Lillian, do this for me, and the debt will be gone."

Lillian went silent, her face still with surprise. She went back to her seat and eyed him skeptically. "You mean that?"

The bounty hunter nodded. "You do this, and you won't see me coming to your door for anything ever again. You got my word."

Lillian snapped her fingers. The veins slackened their grip and let Hawthorn's limbs go. He came over to her.

"I know you want to protect what belongs to you, Lillian. I understand that. I've got my own reasons for needing what Gordonson took from me, but you'll find that yours and mine reasons are much in the same. Which is why I'm asking you to do this for me. And why it is the last time you'll ever see me knocking on your door."

She looked out the window for a moment. "If I were to do it, what exactly do you plan on doing to them? To Gordonson?"

"Giving that screw-brained feather-bag of a dandy a message he won't forget."

She put a palm to her forehead and shook her head. "It'll make me an enemy."

"No. When I'm done with him, he'll stay clear of you and this place like it's a damn hexback pit. He won't touch you or your girls, unless he wants to have my gun barrel shoved down his craw."

She buried her face in her hands and heaved out a sigh. Then she looked up

at him, her green eyes meeting his mismatched ones. "Alright." Then she made a bit of a frown. "Though, I will miss our little adventures."

Hawthorn lit a cigarette. "Yeah."

XII. The Ruse

"I must say, colonel, you take the standards of humane conditions for prisoners to new heights," Dance said, sipping his whiskey.

"Well, I do like the sound of being called humane," Gordonson said, taking his big cigar from his mouth and letting the smoke out through his nose. "Care for another?"

"Don't mind if I do." Dance said, lending his glass so the colonel could pour the smooth brown liquor.

Dance took a hard swallow. "That is good."

"The best," Gordonson said. He watched as the thief took another swig. "Now, Dance, I hope I haven't lured you to think that this little meeting was just so we could laugh and drink."

Dance put down his glass. His face went serious. "I had my doubts."

Gordonson chuckled. "Good. You're as smart as they say you are. Smart as a fox!"

"Then what is your intention for this little chat?"

"It concerns a mutual friend of ours," he said, then took another drag of his cigar, coupled with a swig of whiskey.

"Hawthorn," Dance said, bitterly. "He's hardly a friend of mine."

Gordonson smiled. "And there's a point you and I see eye to eye on. I've got a proposal for you, Dance."

Dance finished another swig. "I'm listening."

"You tell me what it is you stole from Redemption, then show me where you hid it, and I'll be sure to...put some distance between you and the law, enough so

you won't have to worry about wearing a hangman's necktie for a while. What do you say?"

Dance swirled the liquor around in the bottom his glass as he thought. "I see. The enemy of my enemy is my friend."

"You got it there."

Dance finished the last of his whiskey. "It's a funny thing about that saying. In my experience, the enemy of my enemy usually ends up just being another enemy."

For a slight moment, Gordonson's smile wavered.

Then there was a knock on the door.

"Enter," the colonel said, looking away from Dance.

A lieutenant opened the door, a slightly amused look on his face. "Sorry for the disruption sir, but a Mistress Lillian of the Green Ladies seeks your audience."

Gordonson grumbled. "Tell that glorified harlot I have little time, or patience, for her kind."

"She says she has an offer you'd like to hear."

"I said 'no', lieutenant."

"She insists."

Gordonson grumbled. "Damned harlot. Like all other women..." He got up from his chair and straightened his belt. "Let her in."

The lieutenant gave away his eagerness by opening the door instantly. In walked the Mistress of the Green Ladies, dressed in a flowing, button front dress that

seemed to shift from night blue to deep black at every step. Her long red hair was held up in a graceful bundle and topped by a black hat. She flashed such a dazzling

smile it made the heart tingle, and the look in her eyes held enough seductive lure to make any man's loins quiver.

The colonel must have felt the effect, for his frustration suddenly gave away to gratuitous affability. "Welcome, madam. Would you wish to take a seat?"

"Yes, I would. Thank you."

The colonel motioned with his hand. "Well, that concludes our meeting for tonight, Mister Dance. Lieutenant, would you be so kind as to escort Mister Dance back to his cell?"

"Yes, sir."

Without protest, Dance got up from his chair and followed the lieutenant.

"Oh, and Dance." the colonel called just as Dance's boot touched the threshold. "Think hard on that offer of mine."

Dance only smiled. He followed the lieutenant back to his cell.

Gordonson took out a new glass from a drawer in his desk. "Care for a drink, Miss Lillian? I've never known a lady to drink, but it'd seem pretentious—"

"I'll take one, yes."

Gordonson raised an eyebrow.

The Mistress chuckled while running a hand through her hair. "Oh, come now, colonel. You didn't think that because my Sanctuary floats above the earth that I would be above the world?"

"No, I suppose not."

He gave her the glass and poured the whiskey. Gordonson couldn't help but

watch her perfect neck in action as she savored the drink, letting it burn down her

throat. His finger went to the wedding band on his finger. He started twisting it.

She set her glass down. "Colonel, I think it's time I get to the reason I'm here."

"As you wish." The colonel took his seat. To his surprise, the Mistress took his hands in hers. The candlelight gleamed of her lushly red lips and piercing green eyes. He felt his heart thundering, his red blood rushing. He muffled a swallow.

"Colonel, I would like to extend my thanks to you and your men for keeping this town and its people safe."

"Well, it's been our pleasure."

"I'm sure it has. Which is why I thought it only appropriate to give our gratitude in the form of offering my services to you and your officers."

The Colonel chuckled. "I'm flattered, Mistress Lillian, but I recall making it abundantly clear to you what I thought of buying women for the use of their bodies. It's a poison to the mind as much as the body—"

Now she chuckled. She flashed that dazzling smile. "Who said anything about buying? I'm making this offer free of charge, colonel."

Gordonson's eyes bugged open. "F—free?"

"Yes. My girls and I think your men deserve it, seeing that you've been risking your lives against those dreadful Neotok."

Gordonson swallowed and adjusted his collar, his skin prickling with heat all over.

"I—I thought you said you w—were a legitimate business. Why the change of heart?"

She smiled sultrily. "Perhaps I wasn't entirely forthcoming when I described my business, or maybe I've decided to dip my fingers into another bowl. Does it

really matter?" She leaned forward, her green eyes suddenly dazzling, her skin smooth as porcelain, soft as cotton. His senses, his muscles, his very consciousness felt pulled, drawn in, with every motion of her lips, every flick of her tongue. His bones were melting.

"Well—well, I—I suppose not—"

She suddenly leaned forward, her warm breath spreading over his face. Every part of his body shuddered with yearning, his eyes stuck to hers like a fly to wax. He couldn't move, didn't *want* to move. His existence hinged on her; all other things gone from his mind.

"Don't say anything. Only come." she said, running her hands over his arms, to his shoulders, to his neck.

XIII. Sweet Dreams

Fort Greer was made from a mission, a sanctuary for the Disciples of the White and Noble Way. But its bells no longer rung, at least not for White Mass. Cannon batteries stretched their round, black snouts over the walls' tops, and a breach in the ground walls had been replaced by a barricade of palisades made from the surrounding oak population.

Lamps and candles lit the windows and embattlements. Guards patrolled the walls, rifles resting on their shoulders.

Hawthorn waited in a thick patch of underbrush near the palisade walls, not far from the fort's outer well. He heard the sound he'd been waiting for.

The gates to the fort opened, and out rode Colonel Gordonson, followed by several of his commanding officers and Lillian. He smiled. She'd held up her side of the bargain. Now it was his turn.

He crouched low and meandered to the well.

The fort may have originally been built for the peaceful purpose of soliciting the conversion of the natives, but that didn't mean it lacked its fair share of tricks. Hawthorn knew that the Priests of the Way, if ever under threat, would build hidden tunnels underneath the missions to escape the clutches of their enemies. And that's exactly what Hawthorn found once he made it to the bottom of the well. Sure, the water was brimming to his waist, but the torch sconces were still filled. He lit a match, igniting one of the torches, then removed it from its holding.

The golden light reached across the walls and glittered on the still water. His body made ripples as he walked on. He had his belt, bullets and guns slung over his shoulder to keep them dry, along with his cigarette wrappings. Up ahead he could see

stairs made of clay leading up a corridor. His pants sopping, he walked up the stairs.

He came to a door made of oak. He grabbed the iron handle and pushed. As he expected, it opened. Most likely the garrison didn't even know the passageway existed to keep it locked. The door led into a corridor. Candles lit the silent hall. Hawthorn doused the torch and set it underneath a chair, keeping it out of sight. He closed the door and moved on.

If the mission was planned like he thought it was, and he'd been to many similar, the corridor would take him to the cells. He went flat against a wall to let a pair of privates pass. They were smoking and laughing about some joke, oblivious to his presence. He followed the hall further, and at last came to another lined with iron-barred cells.

He crept along, looking in each cell as he went. Most were empty, save for one.

Dance sat there on his cot, reading some penny novel with his legs crossed like he was sitting at home, occasionally fingering the curly ends of his mustache.

Hawthorn whispered to him. "Dance."

The thief looked up from his book at Hawthorn. He didn't seem surprised to see the bounty hunter. "Well, hello there," he said.

"Ain't surprised, huh?"

The thief waved his hand as if to shoo a fly. "Oh, Hawthorn. I think I've learned enough about you in this little partnership of ours to know it would take more than an overgrown vulture, even if it was deified, to bring about your end. Of course, there were the twelve soldiers Gordonson left to make sure the Argentavis had its fill of your flesh. I take it you made quick work of them?"

"You could say that."

"It does seem that Gordonson has escaped your grasp, however. I heard the guards say that the Mistress Lillian made him an offer he found too tantalizing to reject. He's probably tucked away nicely in that levitating Sanctuary of theirs as we speak, along with a substantial contingent of his officers. I doubt your willing to kill in that place."

"You've reckoned right."

"So, what's your plan?"

Hawthorn took a pair of lock picks from his pocket. "It's already working its ways." He inserted the metal picks into the black lock and began picking the tumblers. A series of small clicks followed, and after about five minutes, Hawthorn had the door open. Dance put down his penny novel and stepped out from the cell.

"And from here?"

"I know the way out." Hawthorn took out one of his guns. "But I'm the one following."

Dance took the lead, with Hawthorn keeping the gun trained on his back. With Hawthorn's directions, they made it back to the secret door without alerting the sentries. They trudged through the waterway and climbed up the well.

Once out of the well, they made their way to the horses Hawthorn had hidden away behind some trees.

"Here," Hawthorn said, handing him a canteen once they'd mounted.

"Thank you," Dance said, unscrewing the canteen's cap. "What's your plan regarding Gordonson?"

"I got it figured. It ain't your trouble anyway, Dance. Your trouble is staying

in line from here on till Redemption."

"It wasn't my fault this series of events was set in motion, Hawthorn. You're the one who initiated that brawl, not me."

"I wasn't saying it was," Hawthorn said, wrapping a cigarette. He lit a match, and the flame chased away the scarring shadows set upon by the day's dying light. Soon the moon would show its pale crescent in the ebony sky. The cigarette's end burned.

Dance chuckled. "I'm already seeing something I'll never understand about you, Hawthorn. Gordonson is clearly corrupt, as are most of his men. With your skills, why don't you take a stand and fight his kind, the corrupt leaders and politicians, for the devils and cutthroats they are rather than taking money from them to hunt down the ones championing the right?"

"Is that what you see yourself as, Dance? A champion? I've never heard of a champion that robs stagecoaches and banks."

"The profits of the corrupt. It was bloody before I touched it."

"Maybe so. But my reasons ain't your concern Dance. And I ain't keen on revealing them to the likes of you."

Dance scowled. "As you've consistently reminded me." Dance finished his drink and handed it back to Hawthorn.

"Well, on to Redemp—" On the last syllable Dance stopped and placed a hand to his head. Suddenly, his senses felt clogged with cotton. His vision went murky. He swayed a bit in his saddle, his head steadily drooping forward.

"Oh, my..." He fell onto his horse's mane and lay there, eyes shut peacefully.

Hawthorn smiled to himself, grateful that the sleeping potion had worked. And that his knee was feeling better.

XIV. The Second Time

Lillian had done her job well. Gordonson's and his officers' horses were standing hitched to a pole at the base of the Sanctuary's steps. The white stone of the Sanctuary gave off a ghostly glow under the river of moonlight. It made it easier to see as Hawthorn climbed the steps.

The Ladies had sent home all the lingering customers, save for the soldiers. Hawthorn entered the gate unannounced, then traversed the silent and empty halls. The lavender mist had vanished now, replaced by a faintly bluish haze that hung like a soft bedsheet in the air, with the moonlight sprinkling silver into it. He arrived at the bath hall. He found a circle of ladies there, all of them still dressed in their shoulder-less and flowing green gowns. Lillian stood amongst them.

"We did as promised." She stepped aside, and Hawthorn saw their handiwork.

The strong scent of Opalescence wafted up and all around them. All of Gordonson's soldiers lay in the baths, sleeping and naked, some with eyes so ajar the eyelids vanished behind the balls while others had theirs shut and relaxed. A few even snored. Gordonson was slumbering as well, and snoring like a congested horse while he did it.

"I reckon you didn't overindulge them," said Hawthorn.

"No. Too much of Opalescence can have unforeseeable effects. Some pleasant, but most harmful."

"Good," Hawthorn gestured to the sleeping cavalry officer. "Haul him out."

* * *

They dragged him to a dark chamber somewhere in the deepest recesses of
the Sanctuary. The only light they had originated from a candle sitting on the floor.

Gordonson was awake. He was cold, Hawthorn could tell, and he did nothing but sputter nonsense as he was set in the chair.

Hawthorn watched the man quake and blubber. Gordonson kept looking around and saying something, but it came out garbled and nearly inaudible. Hawthorn thought it may have been a call for help.

No help tonight.

The drug Lillian had given him kept him in this delirious state. But he wasn't so incoherent he wouldn't get the message Hawthorn had planned for him.

The bounty hunter's spurs jingled and his bootheels clacked as he approached the chair. He knelt on his haunches.

"Well, colonel. Seems our paths have crossed again."

He saw the fields again, Hawthorn did. The sun streaking down, its gold cutting across his vision. There was Gordonson, chasing across the field, and Hawthorn's sights were on him. Fires burned in the distance, their black smoke choking out the blue of the sky. Hawthorn fired. He hadn't killed Gordonson then. The shot had been a message. Just like now.

"I want you to listen good, Gordonson. Because this'll be the last time I waste my breath on warning you."

The colonel had stopped looking around wildly and now, dumbly, distantly, focused his attention on the bounty hunter. His eyes were open, but milky and blurry. Tears streaked down his puffy red cheeks. He looked scared, but the look on his face said he didn't recognize Hawthorn's voice.

"I'm not going to kill you like I did that pup and his men you left to watch

and see if I'd die in that gorge."

The colonel started whimpering. Hawthorn grabbed him by the throat and brought the very tip of his knife's blade to rest on the colonel's cock. He felt the big man shiver.

"I want you to know, I want you to *remember*, that for the second time I could've killed you, but I didn't. I had you powerless, my hand around your throat, my knife on your manhood. I took nothing, for the last time."

He let the colonel go. The colonel coughed, making his whole big frame shudder. He started crying now.

Hawthorn left the chamber. Lillian was waiting for him. "So?"

"He's not dead. Not yet."

"Why didn't you do it?"

"Killing twelve men out in the desert is one thing but killing a Republic Cavalry colonel is another entirely." He looked back at the closed chamber. "But God help him if he crosses my path again."

"What makes you think he won't try?"

At this, Hawthorn smiled. "He's a married man and an officer in the Army of the Republic who just willingly tried to buy some love at the Sanctuary of the Green Ladies. If he retaliates, I got enough to sink his sorry ass in the mud forever."

XV. The Object

Dance awoke with a yell as the stark smell stung his nose. The sun's light hurt, and something hairy was in his mouth. He sat up, and spat out the horse hair.

"Enjoy the nap?" Hawthorn said, taking the smelling salts away from Dance's nose.

Dance coughed a few times before answering. "What in hell did you drug me with?"

"A little gift from the Green Ladies. I have yet to find any medicine man or doctor equal to them."

"Yeah. I can tell." Dance spat again. "What is this taste in my mouth?"

"Horse hair."

"No. It's not that. Not that at all."

"Beats me. Let's cut to business Dance. Gideonville and Greer are behind us now, along with Gordonson and his men. Ahead of us is Redemption, and I still need to know where you hid what it is you stole."

Dance sent a wad of spit into sand. "Well, I suppose there's no point in withholding that little tidbit of information any longer. But before I do, I would like to know something."

Hawthorn rolled his eyes. "Shoot."

"You sure went through a lot of trouble back there with killing a deified vulture, slaughtering those men of the colonel's, and liberating me from my cell. Most bounty hunters, I estimate, would've abandoned the effort when faced with such odds."

"Only bounty hunters who ain't worth their salt would've hightailed it,

Dance. I ain't one of those."

"I surmised as much, but the question remains. Is this bounty really worth all this trouble and risk so you can keep me alive until we get to Redemption?"

Hawthorn chuckled. "I don't get convinced easily. You'd better try another tactic for getting me to turn you loose instead of playing on my want for less trial."

"I was curious."

Hawthorn let out a puff from his cigarette. "Yeah, it's that important. Plus, I don't much fancy the notion of having to haul your rotting corpse behind me for another week. Now, back to my question."

"Inevitably."

"Where is it?"

Dance smiled. "With a tree."

* * *

The tree was a little more impressive than Hawthorn had thought. It was an ancient *Segouia* tree, that, despite the ravaged lands around it, managed to keep its cerulean leaves and lustrous bark from peeling away under the brutal heat.

But Hawthorn was wary. "A *Segouia*. You gave it to a *Segouia*."

"Yes," said Dance.

"And how in the great big world did you manage that?"

"Forethought and tact, Hawthorn. Forethought and tact."

"Uh huh."

Hawthorn looked the big and ancient tree over for a little while. The *Segouia* were as old as the sands, perhaps older. Its muted-grey bark which shined with a

peculiar streak of silver when struck by the sunlight was rife with the deep furrows of

primordial age. Hawthorn knew a little of the tales of the *Segouia*, but most of them

had been lost to time. What he did know was that the one *Segouia* before him was probably one of the few of its kind left in the Wilds. And that status made *Segouia* notoriously and aggressively territorial.

"I've heard it said the *Segouia*'s roots reach down to the core of the world itself." Dance said, "thus giving them a connection to the earth that very few creatures of the Wilds ever achieve."

"I'd reckon that. To get close enough to a *Segouia*, you had to bring it an offering." Hawthorn said. "What'd you bring it?"

"Untie this rope and you'll see."

Hawthorn kept his black gun trained on the thief as he untied the rope from around Dance's wrists. They dismounted. Dance took him to a small patch of brush weed. Dance started digging his hands through the sand.

"It's here."

After a few minutes, he stopped. He brushed the sand off gently to reveal a round lid. Dance cut the dirt away from the lid's rim and, eventually pulled the canister out from the dirt. He unscrewed the cap and a luscious aroma filled the air. The familiar scent energy coursing through Hawthorns veins.

"That's water from the Eternal Fountain," Hawthorn said.

"Yes. And it was no easy feat to retrieve, nor to present the water to the *Segouia*. I had to chart the most sensitive areas by tossing stones, and then I only gave

half the water to the *Segouia*. I saved the other half for when I might return."

Hawthorn looked at the water. "You sure went through a hell of a lot trouble to protect something you know nothing about."

"Just because the object is a mystery to me does not mean I do not recognize its value." "Right. Then let's get on with it," Hawthorn said, aiming his gun at Dance. "You're in front."

"Of course."

They went foot by foot, slowly gaining distance, staying rigidly to the path that Dance foreknew. The sand crunched lightly beneath their boots, soft like fabric, yet now it possessed a sensitivity, a strange neural element, that each grain upon which the sand-worn leather of their soles pressed was imbued with an organic membrane, like the feelers on a spider's legs or the antennae on fire ants. They felt every footfall released an echo that went clanging into the earth below, each soundwave shuddering down the length of those nerve-cloistered tendrils. Hawthorn could just see it: thorn-stuck roots poised to rip and rend and flay and dismember their bodies to bloody pulps and ragged flesh. That was one of the few dangers of the *Segouia*.

So, Hawthorn put that much of his trust in the thief, for with death so close, it would be more than mad to attempt trickery while at the bleeding edge. All the while Hawthorn kept his sights aimed at Dance's back, right at the base of his spine. One shot would paralyze the highwayman, that way keeping him alive to reveal the path to the tree. And, without the use of his legs, the thief would be a whole lot less trouble.

Dance spoke. "I figure I should warn you. This *Segouia* is rather sensitive. It knows only me. I don't know how it will take me to me bringing along a guest, especially one such as yourself."

Hawthorn tipped his hat in false appreciation. "Obliged for the warning, but

I'm way ahead of you, Dance. I know about the *Segouia* and their ways. You just worry about getting this done with no complications so we can get on our merry way to Redemption."

Dance rolled his eyes. "Right."

They kept their breath even as they approached the base of the tall tree. Its wind-blasted bark and leaves the color of the grey clouds that heralded a storm-fall towered over them. A strange smell wafted from it, the smell of aging soil and old leaves and lichen encrusted limbs. It tingled over their skin and intruded their senses. Its presence held an aura of ancientness, gleaming and grey, though its edges were frayed black and abysmal with an old rage, an entombed vengeance.

Dance and Hawthorn knelt slowly.

"Get to it, thief," said Hawthorn.

Dance kept quiet as he removed the lid from the jar and poured the water at the base of the tree.

"Here is my offering, sand-worn one."

Though invisible to their eyes, the two of them detected a faint shift in the bark of the *Segouia*. Near its top, a seam cracked open in the old bark. A sheet of the crusty tree-flesh slid away and opened like an eyelid, revealing a large eye, its iris the color of desert orange and rippling faintly like the surface of a lone watering hole, its pupil slit and dark as the inside of a sunflower. It looked at the two of them with what looked like disinterest.

"Ah, the *murthrun* called Dance. You have returned." Where the voice came from the tree, neither of them could tell, but every note and syllable brought with it the sound of leaves rushing in wind and falling to the yellow grass, left to decay and

feed the earth, of seeds sinking into soil with shells cracking and bursting into saplings of wheat or corn, of rain drying on the smooth-surfaced sand but sucked up into the core of the devil-horn cactus with its crimson flowers budding from its arms.

"You brought me what I asked for in return for guarding your trinket...along with a guest." The *Segouia*'s eye lingered on Hawthorn.

"Yes, old one. He's a...partner of mine and he expressed to me his desire to see you and witness your ancient glory before I parted with what is mine."

"'A partner' you say. Then why is his weapon drawn?" There was a change in the ancient tree's tone; wildfires coiling and eating away at limbs and roots and bark, bitter winter winds whipping through leaves and starving away their color, rivers flooding over their banks rising to monolithic deluges upheaving trees, wiping out crops, decimating houses.

The sand around them shifted. Roots broke the surface, grey and cracked from dryness, but ingrained with fathomless strength nonetheless.

Dance tried quick to find an explanation. "He...was afraid that—" The roots were like cords of steel as they grabbed Dance and Hawthorn by their legs and arms, restraining them and pulling them flat to the earth. Hawthorn shouted as his gun fell from his grip and was knocked far out of his reach, while several roots snaked into his holsters and removed his other weapons, including his knife. They did the same to Dance.

"Afraid of what?" said the *Segouia*. "That I might uncover your plot and foil it before it came to fruition? Many have tried in the past to cut me down and steal what magic and ancient power dwells in my roots and limbs and leaves."

His chest flat against the sand, Dance strained his neck to look up into the

Segouia's . "Please. That was not our intent—"

The limbs pulled like the chains of a rack. The two of them grunted, trying to resist. Dance felt the veins bulging in his neck and forehead, his back and chest muscles stretching, head locked in place. He spoke through clenched teeth, eyes glued on the *Segouia*. "I—I kept my end of the bargain."

"So, you did, as far as the Water from the Fountain. But I said nothing about you bringing guests."

"Ancient One, I mean no harm to you," Hawthorn said, himself glaring at the *Segouia* with his mismatched eyes that burned in fury.

The *Segouia* placed its black slit-pupil on the bounty hunter. "I am not a fool, *murthrun*. I have seen the shift of many sands, weathered sandstorms large enough to blot out whole flatlands, withstood cyclones that could uproot mountains. My bark is heat and drought born, my roots as hard as the stone of the mesas, my leaves and limbs dry as sun-washed bone. I reach down into millennia past, to the pools of

crystal in the depths of the earth that have stayed untouched for time beyond measure. I am the writhing howl of the Blindstorm, the lusting gaze of the vulture, the torrent and force of a flashflood. I am one with the desert, a branch of its relentless nature. What makes your word worthy of my notice?"

Hawthorn smiled. "Because I give it, as one creature of the desert to another."

The *Segouia's* great eye narrowed a bit with its barky eyelids. "Speak clearly."

"Look into me."

Dance watched through his pain in disbelief as the ancient tree brought Hawthorn so close to its eye that that its orange color painted Hawthorn's face, while

the hunter's green and red formed two pinpricks, like two precious stones shining from beneath the surface of an apricot lake, in the *Segouia's*. A long moment passed between them, like silent words were being spoken. A peculiar look inhabited Hawthorn's face, like his mind had left his body. The roots suddenly slackened. Dance and Hawthorn collapsed to the sand as the roots released them and slid back beneath the sand.

"I see," the *Segouia* said, his gaze going beyond them.

Dance spat and choked as the coolness of a shadow arched over his back and up his neck. Branches reached down from the treetop, wrapped around

something: a black, almost egg-shaped object about two feet long. It descended and stopped right in front of Dance's nose. Dance placed his hands at the base of the object. The branches unraveled themselves and retreated into the treetop.

"Here is what you came for," said the *Segouia*.

Dance held the object in front of him, as if examining its shape for the first time. After going through so much to get it back, it seemed to have attained a new value.

Hawthorn came to his side. "That's it?"

Dance got to his feet. "It is."

"Doesn't look like much."

"Appearances can be deceiving, Hawthorn."

Hawthorn took the object in his hands and rubbed his hands around the smooth, obsidian-colored surface. It had the coolness of refined steel, yet the softness of clean sand. The object's surface was seamless, flawlessly crafted, almost alien in its perfection. Until Hawthorn's hands struck something, a kind of indention near the

top. The top of the egg split into four segments. Out of the top came a cylinder, made of transparent glass plates and fastened by two circular, silvery metal rims. Strange glyphs that weaved, flowed, spun and glowed with a dim blue aura were inscribed into the metal fastenings. And in the center of the cylinder, held by four needle-thin brackets, was a diamond shaped crystal that glowed with an inner-white light.

"What in hell?" Hawthorn said.

He pressed the indention again, and the cylinder slid back inside the casing as the segments sealed the opening.

"This is what you stole from Redemption?"

"Yes."

Hawthorn stared at it for a moment more. *Never seen anything like it, but these markings...* Hawthorn stored the thoughts away. *Another mystery for another time.* The bounty hunter tucked the object under his arm. "Let's get moving. Lead the way," he said, drawing his gun once more on Dance.

The thief grumbled something as they walked away, a gun pointed to his back. They had only taken a few steps before the *Segouia* spoke again.

"Hunter,"

Hawthorn turned, silent.

"Remember, you gave me your word," said the ancient tree, before his great eye shut, sealed seamlessly away behind bark-flesh.

"What did he mean?" said Dance.

Hawthorn stuck a cigarette between his teeth and lit it, the smoke shading over his face as it plumed up and around the brim of his black hat. "Keep walking,

Dance."

For news and updates on the next installments in the Tales and other works, visit Clark Omo's page on Facebook at @WritingsClarkOmo, Twitter at @omo_clark, and Instagram at arcaneeagle96, or shoot the author an email at clarkpresomo@gmail.com.

Website forthcoming.

About the Author

Texas-grown and Texas-twisted, I write from the heart of blood, sweat, pain, and absolution. The words which I etch into the parchment are not my own but are those I found heaving and writhing under corded barbs, biting into their pinkish, raw-moist flesh, that bound them in the blackest depths of the ceaseless void. I merely released these selfsame utterings of the beyond from their bindings, and they now sing and chant in sacrilegious harmony to those whose dwellings lie across from the dimension of the strange and unknowable, whose minds swim in dark and unfathomable abysses, and whose footsteps carry them past the edge of sanity to the exordium of the cosmos.

Enter now the forbidden reliquary and accursed archives. Tread upon the burning sands of the afflicted wastes and sulphureous barrens. Bow beneath the ancient and unwavering shadows of colossal, featureless monoliths and glimpse the obscured forms of hulking behemoths through the swirling dust and whispering mists. And climb the jagged teeth of the merciless and uncaring mountain so you may reach the hallowed summit where you can lay but only a fingertip upon the cracked stone of the primordial dais that once seated the last, celestial vestige of the divine.

I also drink coffee, pet the chin of my black cat, sing along to The Man in Black, play RPGs and FPSs, read books with plenty to say (along with the occasional forbidden tome) and rewatch *Star Wars*, *Lord of the Rings*, and *John Wick* religiously.